A Song and Puzz

Twinkle, Twinkle, Little Star

Highlights Press
Honesdale, Pennsylvania

Twinkle, twinkle, little star,
how I wonder what you are!

2

Hidden Pictures®

Can you find these 10 hidden objects?

parrot

pot

shoe

oar

cherry

paper airplane

lunch box

candy cane

broom

carrot

Up above the world so high,
like a diamond in the sky.

Draw lines to match
the words that rhyme.

Star   Sprinkle

Sky   Car

Space   Night

Bright   Race

Twinkle   Fly

Illustrated by Claudine Gévry

Illustrated by Liz Goulet Dubois

peanut

gift

heart

boot

pencil

kite

ladybug

Hidden Pictures Can you find these 8 hidden objects?

duck

5

Twinkle, twinkle, little star,

How are these pictures the same?

How are they different?

key
teacup
baseball bat
ring
tack

counting down, then blasting off.

Illustrated by R. Michael Palan

Hidden Pictures®

Can you find these 14 hidden objects?

Use crayons or markers to color in the scene!

toothbrush

banana

caterpillar

pencil

sock

comb

pizza

book

lollipop

Up above the world you fly, in a rocket in the sky.

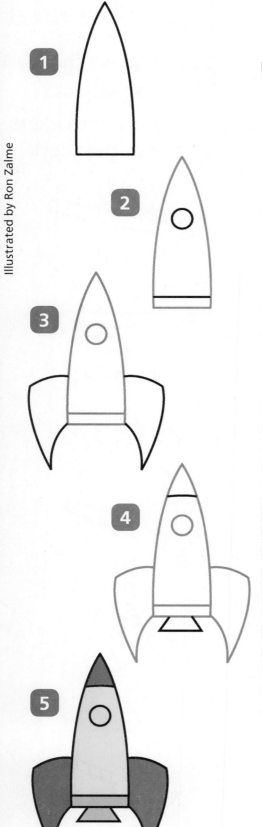

1
2
3
4
5

Follow the steps to learn how
to draw a rocket ship,
or draw one from your own head.

heart

pencil

basketball

baseball bat

magnifying glass

boot

doughnut

ring

Illustrated by Kelly Kennedy

Hidden Pictures Can you find these 8 hidden objects?

Hello, hello, astronaut, counting down, then blasting off.

START

Help the astronaut get to the space station.
Which path will take her there?

FINISH

Good-night, good-night, glowing moon, shining like a big balloon.

Draw a face on the glowing moon.

Illustrated by Maggie Smith

14

envelope

knitted
hat

trowel

arrow

boot

toothbrush

mitten

artist's
brush

Illustrated by Maggie Smith

Hidden Pictures® Can you find these 8 hidden objects?

Sometimes quarter, sometimes blue, sometimes you're a crescent, too!

How many letter **L**'s do you see?

Do you see something that rhymes with "moon"?

Good-night, good-night, glowing moon, shining like a big balloon

Illustrated by Jennifer Bell

18

Hidden Pictures®

Can you find these 10 hidden objects?

ribbon

safety pin

purse

top

bowling pin

necktie

shoe

chair

feather

comb

Alien from way out far,
how I wonder what you are!

Each alien has a match.
Can you find all 8 pairs?

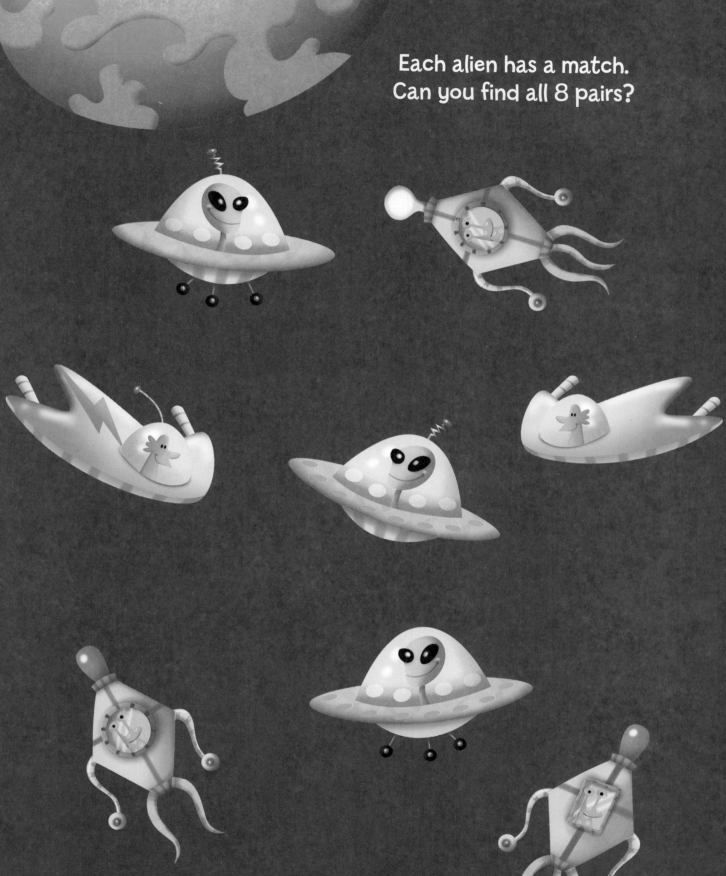

Spotted, green, and slimy nose,

How are these pictures the same?

tentacles, and fifteen toes.

How are they different?

Alien from way out far, how I wonder what you are!

Use the objects in the key to fill in the code and solve the riddle.

What songs do aliens sing?

CODE KEY

P	S	E	T	U	N

Which alien is traveling
to the purple planet?

Hello, sun up in the sky,
shining bright from way up high.

What silly things
do you see under
the sun?

Illustrated by Brendan Kearney

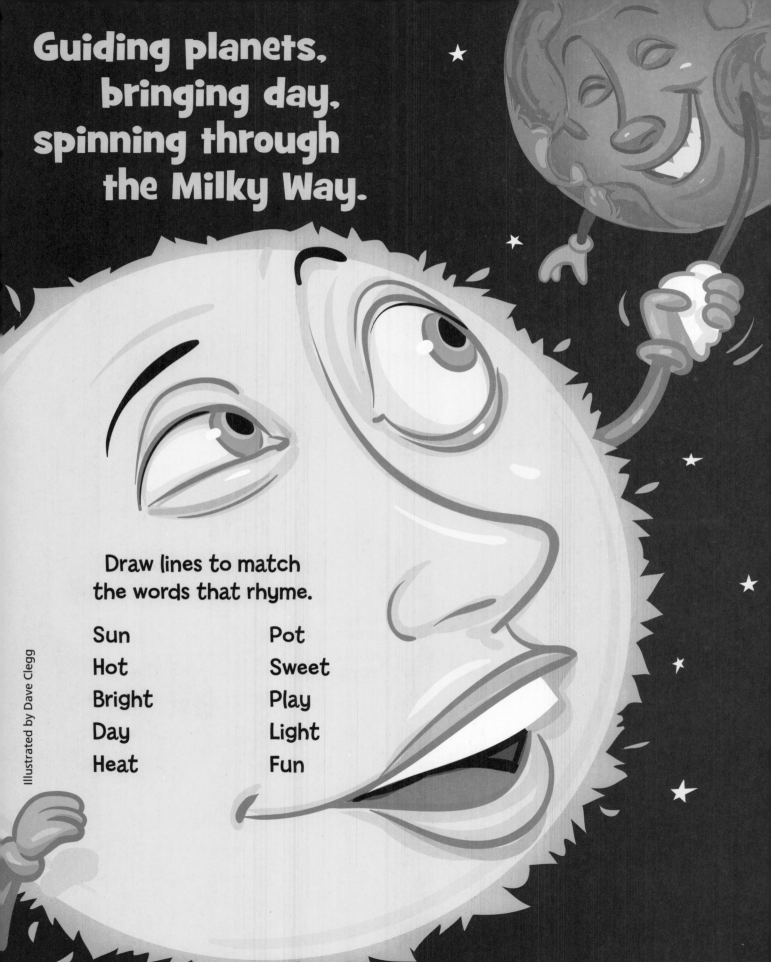

Guiding planets,
bringing day,
spinning through
the Milky Way.

Draw lines to match
the words that rhyme.

Sun   Pot
Hot   Sweet
Bright   Play
Day   Light
Heat   Fun

Illustrated by Dave Clegg

28

magnet

fork

sock

banana

cane

mitten

seashell

screw

Illustrated by Milena Jahier

Hidden Pictures® Can you find these 8 hidden objects?

Hello, sun up in the sky,

Illustrated by Claudine Gévry

How are these pictures the same?

How are they different?

Planet, planet, up in space,
round and round
the sun you race.

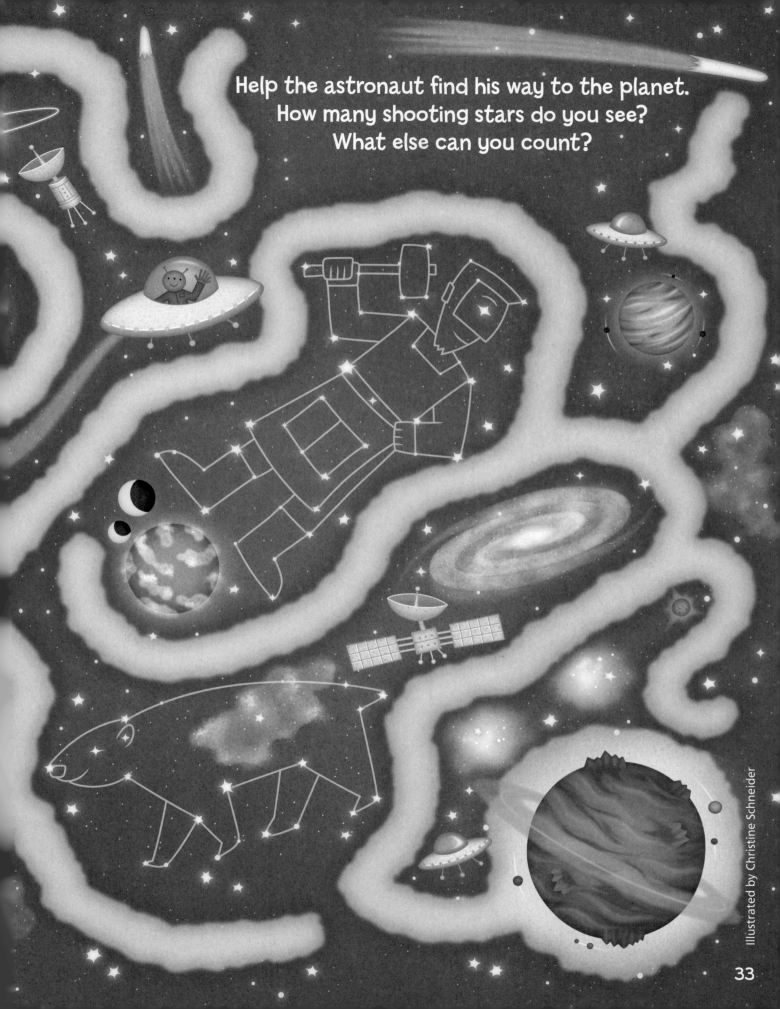

Help the astronaut find his way to the planet.
How many shooting stars do you see?
What else can you count?

Illustrated by Christine Schneider

Saturn, Mars, and Neptune blue,
Jupiter and our Earth, too.

Who am I?
I don't have rings,
But I have spots.
Look for clouds.
I have lots!

Illustrated by Paul Richer

34

What alien do you think would live on this planet?
Use crayons or markers to draw it here!

Illustrated by Jack Desrocher

Planet, planet, up in space,
round and round the sun you race.

hello

USA

What silly things do you see around this planet?

Illustrated by Patrick Girouard

Twinkle, twinkle, galaxy, filled with all these things I see.

Do you see the alien and astronaut?
What else do you see that starts with **A**?

rolling pin

pear

party hat

pizza

button

Illustrated by Patrick Girouard

Hidden Pictures Can you find these 5 hidden objects?

Spinning, gleaming, shining bright,

How are these pictures the same?

twinkle, twinkle all the night!

How are they different?

Twinkle, twinkle, galaxy, filled with all these things I see.

Can you find?
- 5 planets
- 4 shooting stars
- 3 aliens
- 2 moons
- 1 sun

Illustrated by Susan Miller

43

Can you find each of these objects in the book?

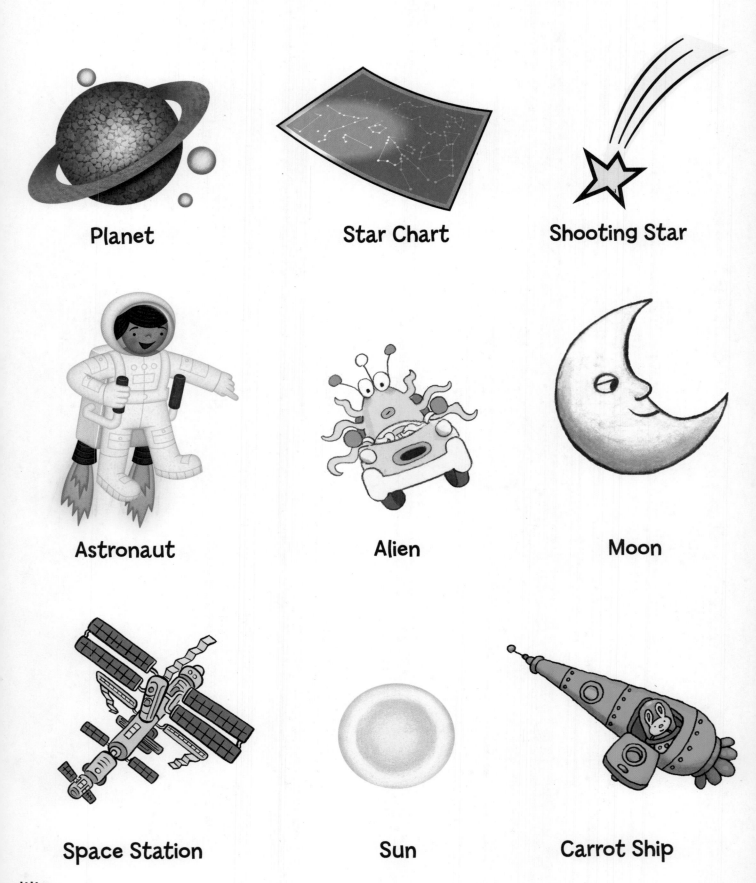

Planet

Star Chart

Shooting Star

Astronaut

Alien

Moon

Space Station

Sun

Carrot Ship

You have found a new constellation!
What is it? Draw the stars and
then connect them.

Illustrated by Mike Moran

Answers

PAGES 2-3

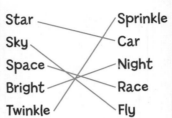

Star — Race
Sky — Fly
Space — Car
Bright — Night
Twinkle — Sprinkle

PAGE 5

PAGES 6-7

PAGES 8-9

PAGE 11

PAGES 12-13

Answers

PAGE 15

PAGES 16–17

PAGES 18–19

PAGES 20–21

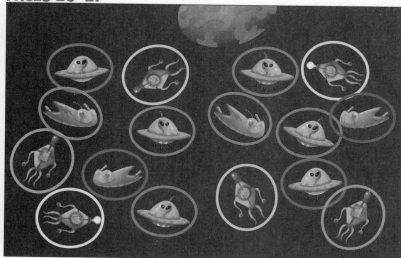

PAGES 22–23

PAGE 24

What songs
do aliens sing?

NEP-TUNES

PAGE 25

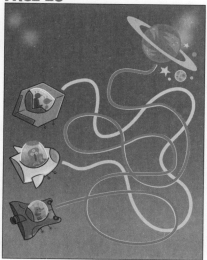

Answers

PAGE 28

Sun — Light
Hot — Pot
Bright — Fun
Day — Play
Heat — Sweet

(Sun→Light, Hot→Pot, Bright→Fun, Day→Play, Heat→Sweet)

PAGE 29

PAGES 30–31

PAGES 32–33

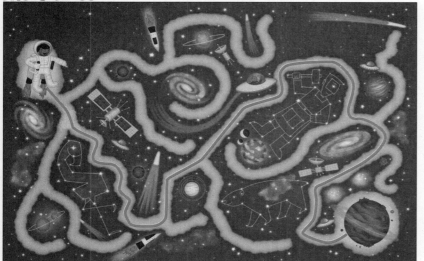

PAGE 34

PAGE 38

Here are the A words we found.
You may have found others.

accordion   anchor
ace   antenna
acorn   antlers
acrobat   ape
airplane   apple
alarm clock   apron
alien   arrows
alligator   astronaut

PAGE 39

PAGES 40–41